DADDY HAD A DREAM

By
Ahmed M. Hamid

ACKNOWLEDGMENTS

This book would not have been possible without the editing support of those with whom I had the pleasure to work during this time, and each of them has provided me with an extensive personal and professional guidance and taught me a great deal about both editing and writing style. I would especially like to thank Professor Jerome E. Goldberg, Ph.D. He has taught me more than I could ever give him credit for here, and he has shown me, by his example, what a good professor and person should be.

Also, my thanks and appreciation to Alex Zeitlin and Keith Kessler, at the Northeast Regional Free Library, in Philadelphia, as well as to my editor, Anthony West, and to Mr. Gene Schneyer, J.D. They all have been supportive of my writing and worked actively to provide me with their valuable efforts and time to achieve my goal and realize my dream of publishing my first book.

Nobody has been more important to me in the pursuit of this dream than the members of my family. I would like to thank my parents, who raised and guide me in whatever I pursue. They are the ultimate role models. Most importantly I wish to thank my loving and supportive wife, Chazza, and our four wonderful children, Shahd, Mohamed, Omer, and Neemah, who provide perpetual inspiration.

Daddy Had a Dream

Copyright © 2018 by Ahmed M. Hamid

All rights reserved. This book or any portion thereof may not be reproduced in any way or transmitted in any form or by any means without the express written permission of the publisher except for the use of brief quotations in a book review.

*To my Dad, who always believed in the
importance of education;*

*To my Mom, who never got a chance to go to school so she
could learn how to read and write;*

*To my daughter Neemah, who always loves to learn and
discover;*

*To my wife, who stayed home to take care of our kids,
so they can continue to learn and develop;*

*To my children: Shahd, who changed my life;
my son Mohamed, who is very kind and full of self-confidence;
and my son Omer, who is using his left hand more skillfully for
writing, thought he is always thinking rightly;*

*And to every teacher and every educator everywhere,
I dedicate this book.*

Ahmed M. Hamid

One night Daddy had a dream.

He saw a bird flying high in the sky, and he said to himself, "We human beings do not have wings to escape the Earth's gravity, but we are very lucky because we have an imagination which can take us anywhere, anyplace, anytime."

Suddenly, Daddy felt something on the top of his head and thought that the silly bird had got him with his smelly white stuff.

But what he felt was my small hand on the top of his head.

I was trying to wake him up. Then he slowly opened his eyes to hear my soft voice.

"Daddy, wake up. It's time to take me to school."

* * * * * *

While he was rubbing his eyes and trying to wake up, I kept looking at the clock on the wall.

"Daddy, can you please wake up? I need to go to school. It's getting late, and my teacher always wants us to arrive on time, ready to learn and participate."

Then Daddy said, with energy and a clear voice, "Yes, Neemah. I will take you to school on time, just like every day, because I know that you love to learn new things, and when you are not with your family, school is the best place for you. There you will always be safe and sound, and that's why we are happy when you are there."

Daddy continued: "So you will not just learn to read and write but you will also build good relationships with your classmates, with mutual respect and appreciation for having good teachers and other school staff members."

Then I said, "Daddy, are you still dreaming? Because you are talking while your eyes are still closed."

Then Daddy held my right hand with his left hand while he was still lying on the bed, but this time with his eyes wide open, and said, "Daddy will get you to school on time, don't worry. But when you come back, even if you want to go to the Moon, or any planets, I will take you there."

I said, "Daddy, I know that you are not daydreaming, and you are not working for NASA, either. How are you going to take me to outer space if I really do want to go there after you pick me up from school? And will we get back home the same day? Because I don't want to miss school tomorrow."

I waited patiently. Then Daddy said, "Neemah, my sweetheart, I need you to remember that, in life, if someone puts his mind into something and works hard, with hope and determination, he will get there no matter how long it will take, regardless of difficulties or distance."

With his eyes still fixed on the ceiling, Daddy continued, "I can put a ladder between Planet Earth and the Moon, and proudly I will carry you on my shoulders. And with one step at a time, we will climb up. No matter how long it will take us, we will get there. Yes, we will get there together, safe and sound."

Carefully I said, "Oh Daddy, how is that possible? The Earth orbits around the Sun while it's spinning around itself, and the Moon is also circling around the Earth and the Sun at the

While Daddy, was trying to wake up, I kept looking at the clock on the wall. "Daddy, can you please wake up?"

same time. I will get dizzy, and who knows what's going to happen, especially with the Earth's gravity."

Daddy then replied with strong voice, "When we weave hopes and dreams from the rays of the scorching sun, and allow the bright light to emanate from our eyes. Starting from the platform of our hearts that are full of love, then sky will be the beginning to where the eye has not seen, nor has the ear heard. That shall be our goal, our destiny. That shall be our promised land."

"Daddy continued, so, let's hopes."

"But Daddy, that is a lot to hope and dream for."Neemah said.

Carefully, and in his deep voice, Daddy answered. "It's only a lot to hope and dream for it if, and only if, we limit our abilities by refusing to go for it. But, it is reachable if we dream it. Yes, my beloved daughter, it's reachable."

Neemah looked deeply into her father eyes and after a long silence she whispered to herself "***Daddy had a dream.***"

She continued to whisper to herself, "His dream is attached to his soul, swimming in the universe and waiting to go home."

Then Daddy placed his left hand on my forehead, seeming like he just red my thoughts and said.

"Yes, those hopes and those dreams are attached to our souls, and somewhere in the Universe laid our destiny, waiting for us, out there. So we're either going to succeed or get caught trying."

Daddy slowly brought his eyes down from the ceiling and focused them on my face. In that moment, I realized I was not "going there" anymore. I was actually "there," on the Moon!

* * * * * *

"Neemah," Daddy explained, "while I am taking a rest and watching you, exploring and picking up small rocks on the Moon's surface, I will also keep an eye on your brothers and sisters down on Planet Earth, just to make sure they are not going to pull away that ladder from us. We do not want to get stuck up here, and you know that I'm not familiar with any schools on the Moon that can teach you--in either English or Arabic, since you are bilingual. If your brothers pull that ladder away from us, I really don't feel like jumping back to Planet Earth just to scream at them."

In his funny voice, Daddy continued: "Also, if I try to jump down to Planet Earth, you know that I have a very bad knee, and maybe on the way down, if gravity accidently pulls me towards the White House, with my African accent they will think I am an alien, and maybe they will shoot me down."

"Oh, Daddy," I said, "you a drama king."

"Not really," he replied. "Life is full of ups and downs, and you must always be prepared."

And then Daddy said, "Sorry, I didn't mean to scare you, but after you finish exploring the Moon and having fun up here, I will take you back to Planet Earth, where Mommy is. You know that she is always kind and she is always cooking yummy food for all of us. There are no restaurants on the Moon to serve us."

Taking a rest and watching Neemah, exploring and picking up small rocks on the Moon's surface.

Daddy then continued, "But if you are in no hurry to go back to Planet Earth, we can go from here to somewhere else."

"Somewhere else? Where is that, Daddy? I don't see any McDonald's or Chuck E. Cheese to go to and play around here."

Daddy thought for a while. Then he said, "From here, if you want, Neemah, we can go to Mars, the Red Planet."

Then I asked, "The Red Planet? Why do they call it the Red Planet? Is it covered with oceans of cranberry juice, or is it full of roses and red rocks?"

Daddy replied uncertainly, "We won't know that until we get there. You decide."

Then Daddy continued, "But from what I hear, the Red Planet contains ice and is mostly covered with red rocks. Besides, it's far away from here, about 48 million miles away from the Moon."

"Daddy, if Mars is so distant from the Moon, how will we ever get there? And if we go there, for sure I will miss school tomorrow," I said.

Daddy replied, "That's true, I shouldn't take my Neemah farther away from home than I already have. And missing school is not an option, so we definitely have to be back before they declare us missing even though tomorrow is Friday and it's a half day."

"Oh, Daddy, you are right, tomorrow is a half day. How come I forgot all about that? But if you can write me a note, I will give it to my teacher when I go back on Monday."

"But Monday is Martin Luther King Day," Daddy said, "and all the schools will be closed."

"Daddy, you are right, all schools will be closed on Monday, but there are still a lot of people in our country who will go out and serve to honor Dr. King's legacy. I heard that he was a

I heard that Dr. King was a good man, he had sacrificed his life for a good cause.

good man who sacrificed his life for a good cause. Because of Dr. King's struggle, the Civil Rights Act was enacted by Congress in 1964 and signed into law by President Lyndon Johnson."

After a moment of silence, I remembered something. "And I already told my friends Sabrina and Amelia that on Martin Luther King Day I would join them to serve by reading children's books about social justice and share quotes from Dr. King that are often ignored by the media.

I went on, "If we decide to go to the Planet Mars, I will miss doing that, and I definitely want to honor Dr. King and keep my promise to my friends; otherwise maybe they will not trust me again." Then I said, "And even though you brought your cell phone with you to the Moon, there are no signals out here. So I will not be able to call them and apologize for my absence if we are not going to be back by Monday."

But while Daddy was looking away towards Planet Mars, he said, "Remember that as long as you are honest and truthful, you will always be able to argue your case and defend it in front of any audience with confidence, and the truth will always set you free."

"OK, Daddy," I said. "If we decide to go to Planet Mars from here, can I serve over there?"

"Yes, Neemah, you can always serve to honor Dr. King's legacy anywhere, anytime. But I am wondering who is going to be over there?"

I exclaimed, "But Daddy, earlier you said that Planet Mars has water in the form of ice. So there must be life, and maybe even people living there right now!"

The Civil Rights Act was enacted by Congress in 1964 and signed into law by President Lyndon Johnson.

"You're right," Daddy said. "Since water is essential for life, any place that contains water might support life in many forms, shapes, and kinds. But whoever we find there, will be a stranger to us. And you know the rules when it comes to strangers."

"In that case, Daddy, we will be the strangers if we decide to go to Planet Mars. And if there are people there. We might be bothering them, so is it worth taking the risk?"

Then I asked, "Why don't we just return to Planet Earth? You can always read me a book about the Red Planet from there."

But Daddy was full of confidence. He said, "We are not going to bother anyone over there. And we can go out there because we are Americans, and we mustn't ignore our identity. Deep in our American soul it is written: We the People always lead the way for an extra mile of creativity and imagination, regardless of the risk or fear. In God We Trust for a better future and we will not stop loving and defending our freedom."

That settled it! I said, "Daddy, I am an American girl who loves her family, her school, and her country. I promise you I will always keep my eyes on our American identity. Daddy, let's roll, let's do it, and walk the walk!" I shouted.

Then Daddy said quietly, "You mean you wish to continue our journey and go to Planet Mars, Neemah?"

"Yes, Daddy. Did you forget, as Americans we always blaze ahead?"

Daddy said, "Yes, we are proud Americans, my beloved daughter, so let's plan on how to get there. First, we are not going to pull our ladder up here and use it for the Mars journey, because that planet is so far away from here. Instead we are going to leave it right here, hanging between the Earth and the Moon, so that when we come back from our Mars journey it will be our landmark to guide us back to Planet Earth, which is our home."

Then Daddy continued, "But from what I hear, the Red Planet contains ice and is mostly covered with red rocks. Besides, it's far away from here, about 48 million miles away from the Moon."

"And as you can feel, here on the Moon's surface we have low gravity. That will allow us to fly in any direction we chose to go, but the only condition is that it has to be the right direction. We can't afford to waste time or get lost far away from Planet Earth somewhere in the fast-expanding universe, Neemah."

My eyes bugged wide open. "What is the *universe*, Daddy?" I asked.

Daddy replied, "According to most cosmologists, the universe was created a very long time ago, and it contains trillions of galaxies, each containing millions, maybe billions, of stars."

Then Daddy continued, with a sad and disappointed voice, "But we really don't know exactly the history and the character of the universe, especially its size, because it is still expanding, in all directions further away from us and faster than the speed of light."

"But, Daddy," I said, "you already knew about the Moon, since you brought me here, and you seem to know about Planet Mars, because we have a plan to go there."

Slowly Daddy said, "No one knows everything, but we belong to a Creator to whom we shall all return. That's why our desire to explore makes us ready to knock hard on any door, and our journey always has to have a purpose."

* * * * * *

According to most cosmologists, the Universe was created a very long time ago and it contains billions of galaxies, each containing Millions or Billions of Stars."

Then Daddy pulled from his pocket an American flag and said, "This is the flag of our Founding Fathers. It is like the one that was brought over here by the spaceflight that landed the first two humans on the Moon over half a century ago. Somewhere around here, it's still telling our story and holding our values."

Daddy kept pointing to the small American flag in his right hand.

"We will carry this one with us to Mars, and so our story and our values will be heard on a new frontier, far away from here. We will leave it there to honor our Founding Fathers, who used their vision to establish the Government of the People, by the People and for the People more than two centuries ago. They fought wrongs, declared independence, and drafted our magnificent Constitution, into which they put their best plans, ideas, and hopes for a unique and strong government like never before on the face of the Earth. Today our government is still guided by those ideals found in the original draft."

"Our Flag was brought over here by the Spaceflight that landed the first two Humans on the Moon over half a Century ago."

Daddy's voice got serious. "Listen, Neemah, to the Founding Fathers' own words," he said. "We seek to form a more perfect Union, establish Justice, insure domestic Tranquility, provide for the common Defense, promote the general Welfare, and secure the Blessings of Liberty for ourselves and for Posterity.' These words are in our DNA as Americans."

After a long silence Daddy said sadly, "After we freed ourselves of the British, a great storm grew within our borders, between the North and the South, and that's when the great President Abraham Lincoln issued his Emancipation Proclamation to end slavery in our country. But that did not come without a fight. For four years there was a horrible Civil War between the North and the South over abolishing slavery and stopping the evil treatment of human beings by denying them their dignity and rights."

In an even sadder voice Daddy went on: "The Civil War threatened not just our unity, but also our very existence as a country. Over one million lives were lost; cities were burnt to the ground. Many families were torn apart and brother was pitted against brother. But despite that tragic war, our ideals emerged victorious, and we managed to preserve our unity and national integrity. And today, almost 250 years later, the state of our Union remains stronger."

After we freed ourselves from British, a giant storm erupted within our borders, and for four Years; there was a horrible and deadly Civil war, between the North and the South, over abolishing the slavery.

Daddy was silent for a few moments, staring into the distance.

Then, with more hope in his voice, he said, "Now it is up to us to carry on that same fight and stand up in the face of any potential challenges, struggles, and injustices. We must continue to carry on the same torch, flaming the bright light of liberty, and now we pass it on to you, Neemah, as you will to your own children someday."

I was amazed by what Daddy had just said. Thinking about it all, I felt proud of my Daddy, my family, my school, and, of course, my beloved country.

Daddy came close to me. He knelt down and gave me a kiss on my forehead and a warm hug so I could not see the tears in his eyes. But I felt his sad sobbing as he held me. When he regained his composure, still hugging me, he said, "Remember that your journey always has to have a purpose."

Then he stepped back and looked at me with his red eyes and asked me, "Are you ready now?"

I replied, "I'm sorry to see you so sad, Daddy, but I promise to make you proud of me all the time, and also I will study hard to achieve my goals and to help others in need."

Then I added happily, "Yes, Daddy, yes, I'm ready now. I am ready to go to Mars. I am ready to fight injustice. I am ready to study hard."

Slowly, Daddy said to me, "Please close your beautiful eyes and take a deep breath."

Daddy came close and knelt down, gave me a kiss on my forehead. Then a warm hug, so I could not see the tears in his eyes.

Then he added, "Continue to keep your eyes closed while taking a deep breath and let me hold your hands."

Then he asked me one last question: "Do you remember what is written in your DNA?"

"Yes, Daddy," I replied. "I do remember what is written in my DNA."

"We the People always lead the way; we go the extra mile, with creativity and imagination regardless of any risks, fears, or intimidations. In God We Trust for a better future, and we will never stop loving and defending our freedom."

* * * * * *

Slowly, I heard Daddy saying "Please close your beautiful eyes and take a deep breath." Then he added, "Continue to keep your eye closed while taking a deep breath and let me hold your hands."

Postscript

As far as the eye can see, and as much as the heart can take, and while I was still looking down at Neemah's beautiful face, I said to myself, "It's true. That was the journey, and that was the dream. What a long way we have come, what a beautiful soul!"

Neemah always inspires me about tomorrow, by always asking me to take her to school on time.

So now I must get up and take her to school on time.

Made in the USA
Middletown, DE
13 November 2023

42570612R00020